T0198768

Fertile Love:
The Magical Story of How YOU Were Made

by Debra Doubrava, PhD

Illustrated by Nicole Smith-Merry, MS & Julia Barry Parker

Balboa Press books may be ordered through booksellers or by contacting:

Balboa Press
A Division of Hay House
1663 Liberty Drive
Bloomington, IN 47403
www.balboapress.com
844-682-1282

Illustrated by Nicole Smith-Merry, MS & Julia Barry Parker

ISBN: 978-1-9822-7732-1 (sc)
ISBN: 978-1-9822-7733-8 (e)

Library of Congress Control Number: 2021923218

Print information available on the last page.

Balboa Press rev. date: 01/19/2022

Foreword

As a psychologist with over 20 years of experience helping prospective parents prepare to use fertility assistance in their quest to have children, I am thrilled to see *Fertile Love: The Magical Story of How YOU Were Made* by Debra Doubrava, PhD. I recommend the reading of books as a helpful way to introduce children to their own story. This book, with its simple narrative and whimsical, brightly colored illustrations, offers an opportunity for parents and children to have a gradually more detailed discussion of the fertility journey and the magic and love that helped bring a very special being into the world.

—Joan L. Bitzer, Psychologist

Fertile (adj.) bearing in abundance.

Dedicated to Gretchen and to families everywhere
who are made by fertile love.
May YOU all live abundantly ever after!!!

Once upon a time (by the way many truly magical stories begin this way and this truly IS a magical story)...

two people fell in love and their love
grew and grew and grew, becoming so big
that the couple's hearts could not contain it.

3

And they knew they wanted a baby to share

their fertile love with.

But try and try and try as they might,
they just could not get the baby recipe right.

The couple grew frustrated wondering if
they should let go of their fertile dream.

Until one day, they had a magical knowing that they needed help

8

to make the baby who was knocking on the door to their hearts.

And so, with courage and fertile hope, the couple asked for help

from angels who were always destined to be part of this magical story.

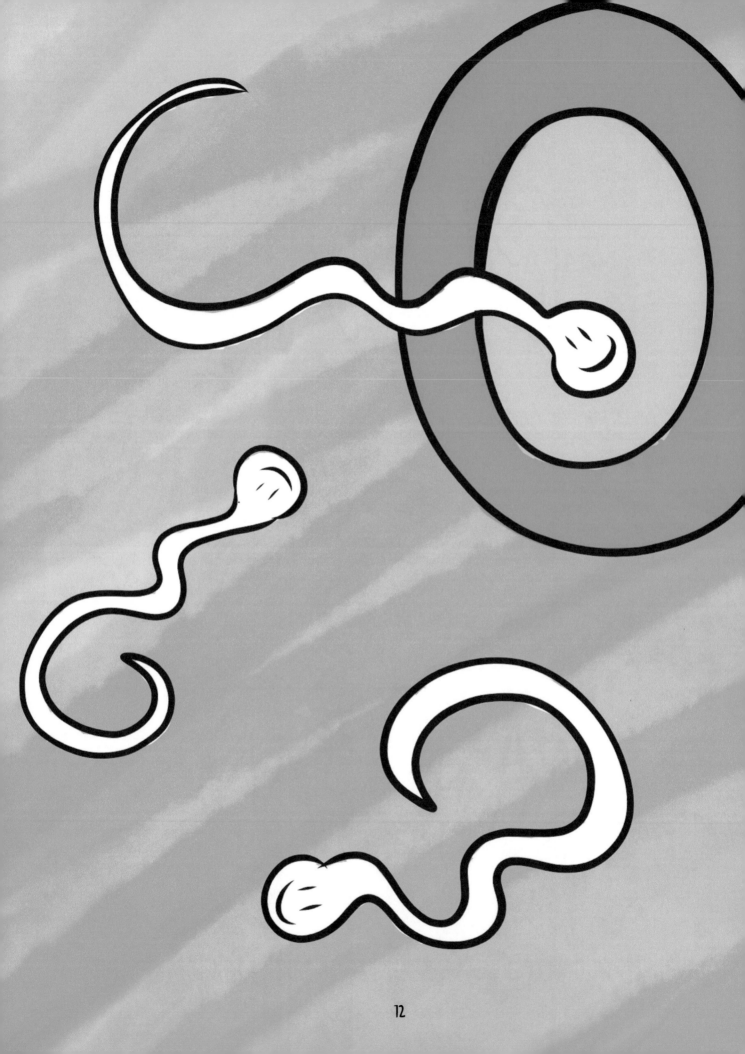

And YOU were made!!!

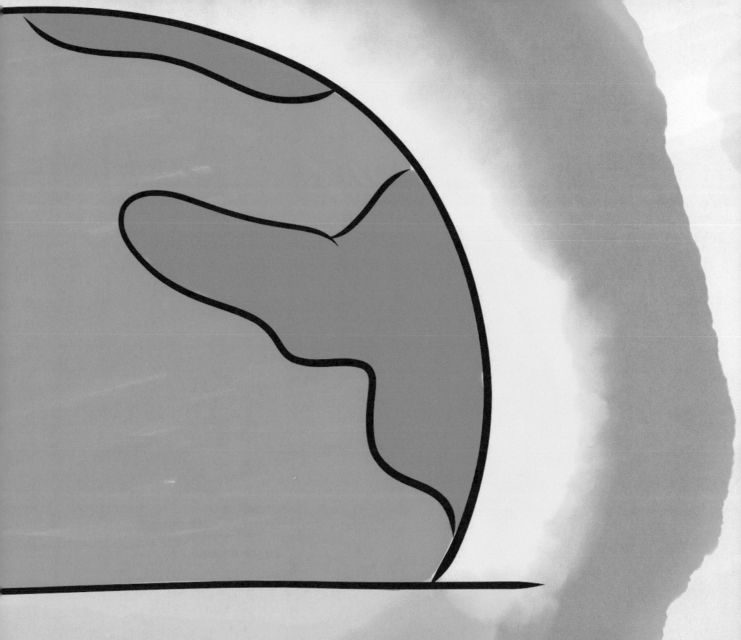

And the couple felt blessed and grateful
to be your parents and like
all was right with the world.

And you will grow and grow and grow.

And your spirit cannot be contained.

And you will live

abundantly ever after knowing. . .

You are MAGICAL.

You are wanted.

You are loved.

THE END

(Many magical stories end this way,
but this is not THE END. . .
it's YOUR beginning.)

Welcome to your life,

little one!!!

Dear Parents:

You did it!!! With help, hope, and love you transformed fertility challenges into the EXACT recipe needed to make your little one. Everyone wants to know where they came from. . .And what a truly magical story you have to share with your child!!!

The abbreviated edition that follows is an opportunity for you to creatively personalize this book for your child's delight and information. Enjoy!

Peace and love,
Dr. Debbie

Fertile Love: The Magical Story of How YOU Were Made in 3 Creative Chapters

Chapter 1: Once upon a time two people fell in love. . .
And they knew they wanted a baby to share their fertile love with.

Your parents:

Three cool things about your parents and their love story:

1.

2.

3.

Thank you, Angel Helpers, for helping to get the baby recipe JUST right:

Chapter II: And YOU were made!!!

Date and Location of IUI or IVF:

Date and Place of Birth:

YOU were named:

    Because:

Three fun facts about your birth story and the making of YOU:

1.

2.

3.

Chapter III: And YOU will live abundantly ever after knowing. . . You are magical. You are wanted. You are loved.

Celebrations of YOU:

Your circle of love includes:

Three magical phrases to describe your spirit:

1.

2.

3.

This is not THE END. . .it's YOUR beginning.

Your parents truly love this photo of YOU!!!

Epilogue: Words of fertile love and abundant wisdom from your blessed and grateful parents to YOU.

Dear